THE BARN

A NOVELLA MYSTERY

BY

DOUG CAMPBELL

AND

JOHN CASEY

PHiR Publishing
San Antonio

Copyright © 2022 by Doug Campbell & John Casey
Cover design by John Casey

All rights reserved. No part of this book may be reproduced without permission. If you would like to use material from the book (other than for review purposes), please contact permissions@phirpublishing.com.

THE BARN is also available in all digital formats, distributed by PHiR Publishing and available wherever e-Books are sold.

PHiR Publishing
San Antonio, TX
phirpublishing.com

ISBN: 978-1-7370627-8-3
Library of Congress Control Number: 2022902509

Printed in the United States of America

ALSO BY JOHN CASEY

DEVOLUTION
Book one of The Devolution Trilogy

EVOLUTION
Book two of The Devolution Trilogy

REVELATION
Book three of The Devolution Trilogy

RAW THOUGHTS
A Mindful Fusion of Poetic and Photographic Art
(with photographer Scott Hussey)

MERIDIAN
A Raw Thoughts Book
(with photographer Scott Hussey)

"The bad ones, the deep, dark secrets, stay hidden the longest. Festering, roiling, gnawing."

—From John Casey's poem 'Skeletons'

ONE

He was uncomfortable during the 30-minute drive to the airport. Because he hadn't slept well the night before? No... Then guilt, perhaps. Long suppressed and only now breaking through some visceral barrier constructed by his subconscious an unknown time ago. Things undone, things left unsaid. Keith left New England to pursue his dreams years ago, and he never looked back. Perhaps he should have.

He took his eyes off the road momentarily to glance at the sepia-faded picture of his mother laying on the passenger seat. In less than seven hours, Keith Conway would soon be back in his hometown to see her and his brother John once again.

A reunion was well overdue. Keith hadn't visited since he took the job with ExxonMobil. Eight years of trudging bleak, expansive landscapes on a multitude of extended trips to Nigeria from Houston. Week after week, month after month of crunching mountains of resultant data. Until one year turned to the next, and the next. He couldn't believe it had been this long. It took a call from his brother telling him of their mother's decline in health to finally prompt his return to New Hampshire.

The silence had been the hardest part for John. He was the sensitive one. Their mother had become progressively withdrawn over the years. Little by little, dementia robbed her of her reason, her personality, and then seemingly (and maliciously), her soul. When he visited it was more to converse with the nursing staff about her condition than to interact with her. Much of the person she had once been was now gone. He would sit next to her as she lay there, staring blankly at whatever mindless program emanated from the small television mounted near the ceiling on the wall.

The entire staff there loved her. Though she was quietly losing touch, much of the time in some faraway world known only to her, she smiled often and never caused any trouble. On very rare occasions of clarity, she would ask about their families and how their days were going. They called her *Sweet April*. John visited at least twice a week, always hoping to catch her on a good day. He remained thankful his small-town job gave him the flexibility to take time from work when needed. Unfortunately, the last few weeks had seen her health worsen. Then a rise in her blood pressure. She fell twice during that time, hitting her head at one point, and bad enough to require stitches. John called Keith and asked him to come home.

TWO

Keith arrived in his rental car. A two-hour drive from Boston Logan to Clarkstown, their boyhood hometown. John never left, never able (or unwilling?) to pull the trigger and pursue his dreams. Once their mother could no longer care for herself, he canceled his lease and moved in with her. His grandmother's house was old, large, and majestic in that colonial New England way, with white wood clapboards, a high-pitched, dormered roof, and a grand brick chimney on either side. Their grandparents, endlessly investment-savvy, converted a little less than half of it so many years ago into two apartments shortly after purchasing the estate. The extra income covered the house payments early-on and more recently, for their mother's care. After her mother died, April managed the apartments, but did not move in right away. Once it became too much of a burden to take care of two homes, she downsized and took up residence once again on the Conway Farm. Shortly thereafter, she began to succumb to dementia.

Neither brother had married. A psychologist might have concluded it was because they were both afraid something terrible would happen. That tragedy ran in the family. And what better way to prevent that than to forego a family?

Keith shut the car door as John strode up. They embraced strongly, each boyishly clapping the other on the back.

"Such a great money maker, this house," Keith quipped. "Are you sure you are not making more than me?"

"Hahaha, I wish," laughed John. "Both apartments have been empty for a while now. I'm thinking about lowering the rent to generate some interest." He dropped the smile and feigned concern, looking at his watch. "For Pete's sake, Keith, you are two hours late! Where the hell have you been?"

"My flight was delayed. Sorry, I should have called to let you know. Great to see you bro. I've missed you."

"Good to see you too," said John. "Glad you made it safe."

"Thanks. So how's Mom?"

John's smile faded. "Not well. It's good that you came. I'm not sure how much time she has left."

"When can we go see her?" asked Keith.

"We'll go first thing in the morning. She is most likely sleeping now, and she needs it."

Clarkstown was known for its farming. The Connecticut River snaked its way through the area, feeding the rich, black soil. The house stood on nearly a hundred acres, some of it wooded. Old stone walls marked the borders of the property and were high enough to keep cows that once grazed there from roaming off. Here and there one could find evidence this was once a thriving farm. In the distance, an ancient red and brown-rusted tractor with sun-bleached, dry-rotting tires stood out stubbornly. The white wooden fences Keith remembered were now gone, but the barn remained.

THE BARN

John made them a quick dinner of sandwiches and salad, and they talked. A steady back-and-forth of nostalgic childhood stories. After a few drinks, the conversation turned to their father. There was very little to remember; he left when they were just toddlers. There were years when they would receive birthday cards, brown butcherblock paper-wrapped presents in the mail for Christmas. But by the time they were in their teens, the letters and gifts stopped. The last John had heard, he was somewhere in Nevada working as a bail bondsman. Keith changed the subject abruptly, telling John about some of his travels to Nigeria.

He acted interested, but to John it felt forced. When the moment was right, he stood up, tossing his white cotton napkin on the table.

"I want to show you something," he said.

THREE

Keith followed John down the hallway to a bedroom he was using as a makeshift office. They went inside, and John opened the closet. It was stuffed with cardboard boxes stacked floor to ceiling. He pulled one out from the top and brought it to his desk and opened it.

"These are all the photos that Mom kept."

John removed them from the box and arranged them haphazardly on the desk. They spent the next hour going through them. Many were pictures of them from their boyhood. Most were older, black and white photos. The picture on Keith's passenger seat probably came from this box at one point. Photos of the house, the farm, Clarkstown, the Connecticut River. Several of Gramp and Gram. Shots of them working in the barn and in the field.

Their mother loved to take photos. Gram and Gramp gave her a camera for her sixth birthday. She would talk about it as if it were the best present anyone had ever given anyone, ever. She took photos of flowers, dragonflies, and all the farm animals. Photography became a passion, and she even had a few published in the local paper. Gramp would send the film away to be developed and in a week or so, the pictures would arrive in the mail, making April's day.

At the bottom of the box, beneath all the photos, was Gramp's high school yearbook. Keith took it out and began thumbing through it. "I've never seen this."

"I knew it was in here, but I've never really looked at it," John replied.

They flipped through the pages and saw their grandmother. Next to her photo was a note from her to Gramp, telling him he was the greatest thing that had ever happened to her. They were married shortly after high school.

There were handwritten notes and messages from all his friends. *'Will miss hanging with you in town Jim,' 'Thanks for your friendship,' 'See you on the other side!'* And many more well-wishing comments from people they never knew. One stood out saying simply, *'I love you,'* in flowery cursive with no indication of who it was from. Instead, there was a small smiley-face sticker next to the note—strange, but cute.

"Who do you think wrote that?" asked John.

"Gram, right?"

Underneath the box they found a few old papers that looked like a lease agreement, and some newspaper clippings.

"Huh. This lease was for the apartment upstairs. Someone named Greg Donovan," said John.

One of the clippings was dated 70 years ago, an article titled *'Tragedy Hits Home, Beloved Farmer Found Dead.'* The whole story, all the facts as Keith and John had always known them, ending in the conclusion their grandfather's death was 'caused by an accidental fall down the barn stairs, causing him to be impaled on his own farming equipment.'

John looked inside the empty box. "That's everything," he said with a sigh.

FOUR

"John, did Mom ever mention anything else about Gramp? I mean, after I left? Did she talk about him at all?"

"Mom hasn't spoken much about anyone, or anything for some time now. Even when she does, it's usually nonsense. I am not even sure if she recognizes me. I can't remember the last time I had what I would call an adult conversation with her. But now that you mention it, she never did say much about Gramp. You know, before the dementia."

They were just finishing breakfast. The photos he and John went through had only strengthened his guilt, each a visual reminder he'd been away too long. Let them down. "What if we asked her about Gramp tomorrow when we see her? Do you think it might jog her memory? She could break out of her haze a bit if we ask her about him. Maybe it would be helpful to her."

"You want to ask her about his death, don't you? Listen, you know everything I know, which is what everyone knows. It was an accident. Why would you want to burden her with those kinds of questions? Why do you want to ask her about Gramp?"

Keith shifted in his chair. "I've been thinking about it more and more. I just want to know who he was. When we were kids, I do remember when she did speak of him, she would say he was such a great man and role model. But that's something we never got the chance to see. To experience. All we have are these pictures..." He hesitated, then continued. "And how he died, John. It was always off-limits. She would never talk about it. You can say all you want about how traumatic it was for her, but I always felt there was more to it. Something she was afraid to talk about."

"Everyone liked him. Everyone. That's what Mom would say," said John. "And dredging up some conspiracy is not helpful. Not when she's like this, brother. I'm surprised at you." He looked at Keith sternly.

He suspected John was probably right. He was being selfish. "I remember. He and Gram were always the life of any party. He was charming. And they loved each other very much. Listen, I'm not trying to cause a stir, just to understand things a little better. That's all."

Their grandfather, James Conway, died on a Saturday morning. Lidya had just come home from the grocery store, calling his name from the front porch to help carry them in. He didn't answer. She managed to open the door without setting the bags down, put everything away, then went out back to see what he was up to. She found him dead in the barn. He was laying there awkwardly, pinned at the chest against the blades of their tractor's sickle bar mower. She always disliked that he kept it there, right at the bottom of the stairs, even telling him once that it was unsafe. To at least drape a canvas tarp over the blades. The entire town was heartsick at the loss of one of their most beloved citizens. Sheriff Clyde Johnson took all of one day to conclude his investigation, documenting his death as a 'tragic accident.'

Lidya was devastated and never fully recovered. In the years that followed she would become more and more withdrawn, rarely leaving the house. Keith remembered his mother lamenting her later childhood years, how in an instant Lidya went from being a laughing, loving mom, full of life, to a quiet recluse, perpetually sad. April couldn't wait to get out of the house. She began dating their father as a senior in high school. As soon as she graduated, they rushed into marriage and rented an apartment on the south side. John and Keith were born shortly after that, then their father left for good, and Lidya died two years later of pneumonia. All in all, their family history was a tragic one.

The town looked up to Jim and Lidya Conway. Jim had made a name for himself as a successful businessman and a fierce negotiator. He knew most every farmer within 200 miles of Clarkstown, and brokered livestock deals all over New England. He was on the road much of the time, scoping out supply and demand. Lydia stayed home, tending to the house and managing the apartments. To all who saw them out and about, they were the perfect happy couple, wanting for nothing. That events would unfold as they did was a jarring shock to everyone in such a tightknit community.

FIVE

Keith and John arrived at Maple Grove, an assisted living facility with a decent view of the Connecticut River Valley. They walked through the entrance and signed into the guest logbook, then proceeded to her room. John had gotten to know most of the caregivers at the facility and appreciated that they cared for her so tenderly.

"Hi Mom!" Keith bent down on one knee, leaned into the bed, and carefully hugged her. He touched her temple gingerly, near the angry red line stitched up from her fall, then stroked her thinned, gray hair. She turned her head and gave him a big smile, clutching a crucifix tightly to her chest with one hand. Keith gave her a kiss on the cheek.

"It is so great to see you, Mom. I've missed you very much," said Keith.

Unfortunately, her only response was the unwavering, but now distant smile. Keith continued to try to talk to her.

Keith went on, compassionately. "Mom, I am so very sorry I haven't been here for you and John. It was wrong of me, and there's not much I can do now except to apologize and promise it won't happen again. I love you and hope you can forgive me."

She stared, straight ahead. Her smile was gone now.

"Mom, say something if you can," John gently urged. "It's your son, my brother Keith—he misses you very much."

They talked to her for a while, both hoping in their own way that somehow, she was hearing them. Then they left, down the hallway to a coffee stand near the cafeteria. They settled in at an antiseptic, white Formica table with two Styrofoam cups of a less than satisfying, weak blend.

"I can't believe she isn't saying anything at all," Keith whispered cautiously. There were several other tenants nearby. He didn't want them to be offended.

"I told you. She's gotten a lot worse since you last saw her. I do think she recognizes you. But for some reason, it isn't processing. Whatever part of her brain that's in charge of reacting or speaking, it's just not working," said John.

"I have to ask her."

"What?" asked John.

"I have to ask her about Gramp. Maybe that will cause her to say something," said Keith.

John sighed resignedly. "I guess it can't hurt. She's not going to say anything, anyway." Then he looked at Keith sternly. "Do not bring up Gramp's death."

They picked up their coffees and went back down the hall to her room. She was laying there just as before, still smiling. John started in again with some small talk, then gave his brother an opening.

Keith walked to the foot of the bed, so he was sure he was at least in the path of her gaze. He locked his eyes on hers.

"Mom, what really happened to Gramp? Gramp Conway. What happened to him? I have been thinking about him. I never believed he fell down those stairs."

April stiffened immediately, gipping her crucifix tighter. John looked at him angrily, then back to her, concerned at the unexpected change in her mood.

Keith did not want to lose whatever attention he might have captured. "You told us a story when I was seven years old, about what happened to Gramp. How he died. Was that the *whole* story? Is there anything else?"

"Keith, *STOP*," John whispered forcefully.

But she remained silent. She didn't have much time left. And when she finally died, with her would go any chance the brothers had at understanding more about the man that friends and neighbors would describe as 100% American. Friendly, caring. Rough, but good looking. And whether or not his death was truly an accident.

A tear began to form at the corner of his eye. It was a combination of seeing his Mom like this, and realizing he would never know anything more about his grandfather. Perhaps it was his own fault. If he hadn't left, or if he'd returned home to visit from time to time, things might have been different. He could have spent time with her when she was still lucid. He could have learned all there was to learn about his grandfather. Instead, he became self-absorbed and distant, too caught up in his career and travels to check in on her as her health declined. He'd ignored his brother as well. The two most important people in his life.

John and Keith looked up as the floor caregiver knocked at the open door and entered the room. He said "hello," nodded curtly at them, then began readying April's room for the day.

"Mom, we'll be back tomorrow," said John. "Keith has to head back to Texas in the morning."

She turned her head toward him, ever so slightly, and smiled again.

Back at the house, Keith got out of the car pensively. "I'm going to take a walk around the property. See what's changed," he said.

"Do what you want to do, you're good at it," replied John. "I still can't believe you brought up Gramp's death. You said you wouldn't. I'll be in the house."

"Sorry. You're right, I shouldn't have," Keith acknowledged.

"It's fine. I'll put a pot of coffee on. That crap at Maple Grove didn't do it for me."

SIX

The once white, now mostly gray gambrel-roofed barn had two sets of wide, double doors, one at either end. Large enough to allow the tractor in and out. Keith grabbed a rusted metal handle with each hand, slid the suspended doors left and right on their rails, and went inside. With no windows on the first floor, it was dark inside. All these years later, and there was still no electricity. He fumbled with his smartphone, tapped the flashlight app, and walked inside.

The barn had been used for storage in recent years and was filled with random junk. A large tube TV console in the corner. An oxidized aluminum ladder hanging sideways on the wall. The card table their grandparents would set up on Sunday mornings after church to play pinochle on with their friends. A pile of wooden folding chairs. He shined the light around. Antique farm tools hung here and there, suspended from square-headed nails in the walls. A two-man handsaw. The metal 'Conway Farm' sign that once stood next to the driveway near the road leaned against the far-left wall.

Further inside, he approached the stairs leading up to the second story. They were still in good condition, a nail head poking up here and there. It didn't look like much from the outside, but aside from (and despite) the hole in the steeple roof, the barn had weathered time quite well. He shined the light all around the base of the stairs, kicking aside the dust and brittle remains of yellow straw. Keith was hoping to see a stain on the wooden floor. Proof of where he died. If there ever was, it had faded long ago.

A noise upstairs startled him. He dropped his phone.

What the heck? Damn it. He picked it up and looked at the screen—it was cracked.

Keith illuminated the stairwell and began to walk up, scanning the area above where he heard the commotion. He caught himself tiptoeing, as if there were some reason to be quiet. Each step creaked long and ominously. At the top, he no longer needed his phone, with sufficient light filtering through the windows and jagged hole in the steeple roof. Then the noise again, closer this time. He nearly fell backwards and down the stairs as a large crow flew by his head and upwards.

"Damn!" he muttered, gathering himself.

Sheepish at being so easily frightened, he shined the light on the rafters above and saw him perched there, head cocked to one side curiously, looking down at him with one glassy black eye. It had always been easy for his imagination to get the best of him, especially when alone and in a dark place.

The second floor was largely open with four partitioned spaces, two of them storage areas for fence building and other materials and tools. The largest area was where his grandparents would store hay for the winter. A small, scattered pile of it still lay there in the middle. This barn held so many memories. Most of them were good, dating back to the days Mom would bring them to visit Gram. Hide and seek, exploring. But now, the run-down, disused building exuded something else. Portentous and foreboding. He shuddered a bit, even though he knew it was all in his head—this was where his grandfather died, after all. But he couldn't shake the feeling.

There was a square, gaping, open space between the first and second level that made it easy to move material up and down and over to each of the rooms. It was essentially a large hole in the second story floor. A waist-high safety railing ran intermittently along all four sides, a four-foot gap in the middle of each. The gaps were there to allow hay and equipment to pass through as it was brought up to the loft. Chains across the gaps could be hooked and unhooked as needed. Two were still in place, the others were missing, broken at some point and never repaired. An industrial-sized block and tackle hung from above through the middle of it, completing the picture.

He'd forgotten how tight the staircase space was. It was maybe two and a half feet wide, left to right. It would be nearly impossible for someone to fall without hitting one wall or the other. And there were railings on each side… Gramp was strong and athletic, only 28 years old at the time. He fell down *those* stairs? How could he have not caught himself?

Above and through the rafters, Keith surveyed the interior of the steeple, with windows on two sides. He wished briefly he could get up there somehow. He would have a great view of the property and surrounding hills if he could.

He sighed and walked back down the stairs, pausing for a moment where the stain on the floor should have been. He said a quick prayer for Gramp, then headed back to the house to have coffee with John.

SEVEN

Later, Keith and John decided to go for a stroll. Their grandparents' was a rare property, prime real estate right at the edge of town proper; walking distance to downtown. Just five minutes down the road, they turned onto Main Street and passed by the Piggly Wiggly, the hardware store, and the town hall. There was nothing much for John to see, but Keith took it all in, noting every little change. The local real estate office was open as they walked by, and out popped Jane Cranmore, one of Clarkstown's most colorful residents. At 75 years of age, she was still very active and never overlooked an opportunity to talk. If the town had a celebrity, it was her. She knew everyone, and everyone knew Jane.

"Hi John!" she exclaimed with an over-eager vigor. "Is that who I think it is with you?"

"Hi Jane, yes, it's me Keith." He smiled, holding out his hand cordially.

"My goodness, I can't remember the last time I saw you! So great you are back in town. Handsome as ever! How is your mom doing?"

"Not too well, unfortunately."

Her expression changed drastically, dropping from a huge smile to an overstated frown.

"So sorry to hear that. My poor boys, I think your mom is such a great lady." Her facial animations were perpetually distracting. She then reverted back to the smile.

"But how are *you* doing, Jane? How is your father?" Keith asked.

"I've been fine, running around town, selling this, selling that. You know, the usual! And good old dad, well he's still kicking."

"What is he, 95 now?"

"Yes, 96 actually. Amazing, isn't it? It's from healthy living, and good genes of course."

Impossibly, her eyes and smile grew wider and larger as she flicked her over-dyed hair to the side, put her hands on her waist and pushed out her hip. It was comical.

John smiled as Keith went on. "Do you think I could talk to him? I'm looking into some of my grandfather's history. I know they were close."

"Oh of course, he knew your grandfather well. He'd be delighted to talk with you. You should come over to my house in an hour or so, he's there, probably napping right now but should be up soon. I baked a zucchini bread last night. Ooh, and I'll make some lemonade! It'll be fun. But first, I have to get some paperwork to the title company."

Keith glanced at John, who shrugged.

"Great, thanks Jane—we'll be there."

"OK, perfect! See you boys in a few!"

She waved goodbye and scampered across Main Street.

John was worried about where this might be going but said nothing, deciding instead to let it play out. After walking home and resting up for a bit, they made the short drive to Jane's house in Keith's rental.

Jane ceremoniously welcomed them inside, a large blue and white Polish pottery plate of sliced zucchini bread in hand. "Dad, our visitors are here!"

Tom was in his wheelchair, positioned next to an overstuffed, floral-patterned recliner. A fading framed wedding photo of Jane and her late husband Michael graced a side table to his right. Jane placed the platter carefully on the coffee table next to a set of glasses and pitcher of lemonade.

"Go ahead boys, take a seat," she said while sliding into the recliner next to her father.

"Thank you, Jane, much appreciated. Hi Tom, you may or may not remember us, it's been a long time. We were both much younger the last time you saw us, I think. Keith Conway and my brother John."

He extended his hand across the zucchini bread.

"Hi Tom, good to see you again," John followed.

"Of course I remember, how are you two? What brings you to our house today?"

He bent over and put a slice of bread on a small plate, his hand shaking visibly.

Keith went on. "Well, I've been away in Texas for several years, and as you've probably heard, Mom isn't doing so well. I came home to spend some time with her and John here. I've also been thinking about other family matters. I know you and my grandfather were close when you were younger. I thought maybe we could talk a bit about him."

"Of course, Jim was a great man and a good friend. I remember him well," said Tom. "What would you like to know?"

"Being back home has led me to reflect a lot about my past. On my family. Our Mom never told us much about him, and she would never speak of his death. I know it was pretty much an open and shut case back then, that he fell and it was an accident. But do *you* remember anything from that time, anything at all? Was he in trouble with anyone, was anyone upset with him back then?"

Tom exhaled and gathered himself. Keith sensed there was something there, something Tom knew.

"Gosh, Keith. Honestly, these days I don't remember much about what I did yesterday, never mind what happened seventy-odd years ago. I do remember your grandfather as a very popular guy, though. Everyone liked him. I was a couple years younger than him, and he was more popular than me with the girls." He chuckled. "In the end, it was Lydia who charmed him. I think I might still have a picture of us."

"I'd love to see it," Keith replied.

"Jane, do you mind grabbing that photo, you know the one? I think it's in the old hatbox, with all the others. Underneath the stairs."

"I don't know about that photo in particular dad, but I'll get the box. Hold on."

"Thanks sweetie."

Jane got up and left the room.

"Tom, do you remember, when he died, if there was anything suspicious about it or about the investigation? Anything at all?" Keith continued.

"Vaguely. I mean, I remember it happening, it was such a shock to me, we were such good friends. I just don't remember the details. I know Lydia came home and found him there in the barn. They claimed that he fell down the stairs. I never believed that myself."

John and Keith exchanged glances.

"What do you mean, you didn't believe it? Why?" asked Keith.

"Well, he was young, and a strong guy. He was athletic, not one to lose his balance. I just can't see how that could have happened. There was something off about it, as I remember. It happened, then the next day it was in the paper, reported as an accident. The investigation was over before it even got started. Now, I'm not trying to say there was some kind of conspiracy, or that Sherriff Johnson was hiding something, not at all. It's just my opinion. I don't have any other information about it, just my gut talking."

Just then Jane reentered the room holding the photo Tom mentioned. "Here you go," she said, handing it to Keith.

"Your grandfather is in the middle," said Tom, pointing.

A group of kids on the riverbank in swimsuits. Tom was on the end, the shortest. Jim Conway, in the middle, was flanked by two young girls. Two other skinny boys rounded out the photo.

"I recognize my grandmother, on his left. Do you know who the other kids were?" asked Keith.

"Let me see. On that day we all went swimming. One of the hottest summers ever, and one of those days I will always remember. That's me, this guy was Greg, Greg something or other, I forgot his last name, but he wasn't in our group for long. Chris Jones—he went on to play for the Sox, in the minors. And Lydia, Jim in the middle, and…I can't remember the other girl's name. I want to say Margot or Melanie. She wasn't really part of the group either; she was a troublemaker. It was the first and last time she did anything with us, I know that."

"Are any of them still alive?" asked John.

"Well, I'm alive!" he chuckled. "I don't think so. I wish your grandmother were still here, she was always so kind to everyone."

"What about the troublemaker?" Keith pressed.

"I just don't know." He paused in thought. Then he raised his eyebrows. "But I do remember she was trying to kiss your grandfather that day. Lydia was so mad. She pushed that girl in the water, and she hit her head on a rock."

Tom sighed. "Then we all scattered. We knew she'd be OK, but none of us wanted to get in trouble. We heard she ended up in the hospital. Ended up having stitches on her head and face. But she was fine. We didn't see her at all after that."

"Grandma one, Margot zero," John said kiddingly.

"Yeah, right, Lydia could be a real firecracker. Crazy things happen in small towns," said Tom. "You can keep the photo."

"Thanks so much, Tom. We're grateful for your time, and for sharing your memories," said Keith. "And thanks Jane for the wonderful zucchini bread."

EIGHT

The next morning, the brothers drove separately. Keith planned on leaving for Boston Logan immediately after their visit with Mom.

Before heading to her room, they quietly shared a bland but hot breakfast and the same bad coffee in the Maple Grove cafeteria. By now, Keith was resigned to the fact he'd never get all the answers he was looking for. He was grateful, however, to have seen his mother again while she was still with them. He wasn't sure there would be a next time.

Once finished, they returned their food trays and walked down the hallway to her room. The visit didn't last long.

"I love you Mom. I promise to come visit again soon," Keith told her warmly.

He lingered, waiting for some response, but none came. Her gaze remained fixated on the television, a 1990s Oxygen Channel tearjerker unfolding on mute. They sat in silence for half an hour.

"You should get going. I'm going to hang out a little longer," said John. Keith agreed and gave April a kiss on the forehead. Then they walked out to Keith's rental in the parking lot.

"I miss you, Keith. I wish you didn't have to leave so soon."

"I'll be back, John. I promise I won't disappear this time."

John secretly hoped that were true. It took nearly a decade for him to return the first time, and Keith would soon be the only real family he had left.

Keith got in the rental, waved, and drove off. Weaving his way south through the traffic on Interstate 93, his thoughts remained on Mom and John. And as he had felt on the drive up, the guilt began to creep back in. He was leaving them again. As if on cue, the overcast sky took on an ominous quality, darkening quickly as droplets of rain hit the windshield. *How appropriate*, he thought.

Halfway to the airport, his cell phone rang. It was John.

"You should come back, Keith. Mom passed away, just a few minutes ago."

Keith didn't know what to say, so he said nothing. Was it possible she held on just long enough to be able to see him one last time? The possibility of it gave him a small amount of joy. But it could not overcome the wave of loss that washed over him.

"Keith, are you there? Did you hear me? Mom is gone. She passed as I held her hand. It was peaceful."

He choked back the tears. "Um, yes, Yes, I'm here. I'm turning around. I'll be back there in about an hour."

"OK. Drive safe brother."

"I will."

Keith returned to Maple Grove. It was a difficult day. They spent two and a half hours with various staff, going through their standard checklists. It felt wrong, desultory. Sterile. It must be hard for anyone working there to keep up the façade that they actually care, thought Keith. Though they had all seemed to take such good care of Mom, it couldn't be anything other than a carefully acted lie. It was a daily thing at these large facilities—old people dying. Dying was their business.

After finishing with the initial arrangements, they drove back to the house.

"Keith, I didn't mention it earlier—the timing wasn't right. But before Mom passed, she grabbed my arm. And she talked to me."

Keith snapped out of his melancholic haze.

"What did she say?"

"It was unnerving, to be honest. She whispered to me, almost as if she were telling me a secret, and didn't want anyone else to hear. She said, *'It's in the barn'*."

"*It's in the barn*? What do you think that means, 'It's in the barn'?" asked Keith.

"I don't know. Maybe nothing. But it was strange. I mean, these were her last words. I guess it could have been a dementia-induced fragment of her memory just running its course. Or, it could have been the one last thing in her mind that had yet to be destroyed by her disease, one final memory she held on to. After she said it, she let go of my arm and pointed up."

"She pointed up?"

"Yes. She dropped her crucifix, held up her hand at a forty-five-degree angle, and pointed. It was strange, to be sure. I felt a little scared, actually. It was as animated as I've seen her in months. Then she went rigid, her whole body."

"You don't think it had anything to do with me asking about Gramp, do you?"

"I have no idea."

NINE

Staying on with John for an additional week felt appropriate. The right thing to do. He wanted to help with preparations for her funeral, and with whatever estate issues needed to be handled. If it took longer than that, John would have to take care of it. He was needed back at work. It was a good thing his boss was understanding. In the meantime, Keith needed to give John as much support as he could offer. At first, he found it troubling that his brother didn't seem to be as affected as he was by Mom's death. With more reflection, however, he realized John was at peace with it. He had been there for her all along and saw it coming. He was able to prepare for it psychologically. Keith was the absentee, the self-serving one, the Kane to his Abel. And thus, he was rightfully marked. His pain was a deserved scourge on his soul that would only be lessened by time.

The additional layover in Clarkstown would give him time to address something else. Mom's deathbed comment had re-catalyzed Keith's sense that there were truths about their grandfather's death that were still buried. He'd acknowledged earlier that his guilt was partly to blame for fueling his inquiry into the matter—that he could never atone for being absent all these years, but he *might* be able to right another wrong, to mend a different family injury that had languished for decades unhealed.

THE BARN

He needed to take another look in the barn. Forensically, this time. Their mother's deathbed statement wouldn't leave his head. *"It's in the Barn."* But what was *it? It* must be significant—these were her dying words, the last she wanted anyone to hear. But if *it* were so important, why would she wait until her final moment on Earth to tell them?

TEN

A sunny day made things easier. He could have asked around to borrow some floodlights, but mother nature was cooperating to the extent that he needed. After Keith slid the doors open, both at the front and at the back of the barn, there was plenty of light. He began by moving all the junk away from the staircase, careful to inspect everything as he did. He piled it all in the far corner. He did have a pretty good flashlight this time, which helped in corners and areas that remained in shadow. When he was finished rearranging, he scanned the first level, methodically. Square foot by square foot. The floor, the walls, each stair. Nothing appeared out of the ordinary.

He used a leaf blower to clear out the dust and debris, blowing half out through the front doors, and half out the back. Only then did he notice a difference. Where he'd expected before that a dark stain should have marked where Gramp died, he now saw something. Instead of a dark stain, though, it was a lighter area. As if the wooden floorboards had been scrubbed with bleach many years ago.

Keith scanned the first level again. From the corner of his eye, he noticed another area that seemed lighter in color, but it was not the same—larger and barely perceptible; they appeared newer than the rest. Three long planks in the middle of the floor, side by side. Perhaps replaced by after the original construction. As he began walking toward them, he lost the visual—they no longer looked lighter. Keith walked back to the spot where he saw it. Whatever difference he'd noticed was now gone. *An optical illusion?* Turning away, he again noticed the lighter planks, again from the corner of his eye. He noted the three mentally and walked back over to them, scuffing each with the heel of his boot so he wouldn't lose them again. If they had been replaced, it was a long, long time ago. And it likely meant nothing—Gramp was always repairing everything; he kept the barn in great shape. It was only after he died that things started to deteriorate.

He looked upwards. The three planks were almost directly beneath the block and tackle hanging through the large opening from the rafters above. It made sense—if the block had fallen at any point, or if something heavy had fallen from its hook, it could have damaged the floor. The floorboards were very heavy, though. Nearly three inches thick, enough to support the weight of the tractor and farm equipment rolling in and out. It was more likely they'd begun to rot, and were replaced. Or, maybe they were just a different type of wood than the rest...

Blower in hand, he made his way up the stairs and used his flashlight to illuminate every square inch of the second floor. But he found nothing. A lone, repurposed chest of drawers that had seen better days stood empty against the far wall. Gramp had used it to store a multitude of odd metal hand tools, the kind you might need once or twice in a lifetime. Again he cleared away the thick layer of dust and detritus, moving it all into a pile near the corner. Then he walked over to one of the railing gaps, where the block and tackle rope was tied off to a post, and he leaned casually against it as he inspected the now-clean floor. As soon as he did, though, it began to give, and he took a step away. Keith noticed it was cracked and had been repaired at some point, years before. A broken piece of chain hung to one side. Keith gazed down through the large square hole, eyeing the three scuffed floorboards below. From this vantage, they looked no different than the others.

He examined the interior of the steeple. A chaotic, almost surreal dance of dust particles filled the air, kicked up by the blower and backlit by sunbeams filtering through the high windows and jagged gap in its roof. He then thought of John's demonstration of their mother's delusional, final moments. Was she referring to the steeple? The second floor of the barn? Or was she simply pointing in a direction she thought was towards her home, to the barn? He stared through the swirl.

This is a waste of time, he said to himself. What was he doing? Still looking upwards, he slowly shook his head, casting his troublesome thoughts aside. He decided he would close up the barn and go help John with the funeral preparations.

At that moment, the dust and sun from the windows made him sneeze, four in quick succession. As the reflex ebbed, he opened his eyes, slightly dizzy. He wobbled near the edge of the opening in the floor, catching himself on the railing. He nearly fell right through the gap. A surge of adrenaline coursed through his veins as he regained his balance.

He was suddenly upset with himself. John was taller, maybe smarter. But Keith was the analytical one, more rational. Procedural. It was as if their roles had been temporarily reversed. He was getting nowhere with this; there was nothing here in the barn that indicated things had happened any differently than what was reported in the paper all those years ago.

He put the flashlight in his pocket, grabbed the blower, and walked back to the staircase. As he neared the top, he tripped on an exposed nail head and fell face down, hard. Rolling over on his back, he did a quick mental inventory of his body—no significant pain. A bump on his temple. He blinked rapidly and laid there a moment. Then something caught his eye. A protrusion under one of the steeple windows. It was only visible because of the angle, blocked from view in almost every other area of the second floor by the rafters.

Regarding it curiously, he got up gingerly and went down to get the aluminum ladder off the wall. He dragged it up the stairs and leaned it out across the pass-through in the floor, setting it against a rafter just below the bottom of the inside of the steeple. Then he began to climb.

Once at the top, he looked over at it, a platform of sorts beneath the west-facing window. The eastward window had a similar, extra-large sill. Large enough for a person to stand on. Maneuvering carefully, he stepped off the ladder with his right foot and moved onto it. The Connecticut River came into view and beyond it, rolling green hills dotted with white homes not unlike his grandparents'. Nearer and just to the south, he saw the neighbor's farmhouse, the second story just visible above the treeline. He squinted. In one of the two windows he caught sight of a still, shadowy, figure backlit by a light in the room. Two hundred yards or so away. It was difficult to tell, but it appeared as if the person might be looking at the barn. Looking at *him*? A shiver went down his spine. It was odd—there was no good reason for him to feel this way. They were probably just taking in the countryside, innocently, as people do. He closed his eyes and shook his head, holding a crossbeam for support. He looked back at the house, but the person was gone, and the curtain was drawn.

Keith shook his head again, deciding then to go back to the house. As he extended his leg deliberately to the top of the ladder, he saw something out of place. He stepped back to the sill and took the flashlight from his pocket, shining the beam towards the corner. Lying on top of a rafter within the steeple framing—what looked like an old Kodak camera.

Bracing himself, he leaned over and grabbed it. He used his thumb to wipe away the dust from an inscription on the back, *April Conway*. Almost unconsciously, Keith half-pointed his index finger again, realizing this was what Mom must have meant. She wanted her camera to be found.

ELEVEN

John scratched his head. "I don't know what to make of it. I don't think that's what Mom meant. I mean, why would she keep it up there, anyways? It's strange."

"I agree, it's strange," replied Keith.

"Seriously, why leave it up there though?"

"A good question...but not the best one." Keith held the camera up.

"Is there...any film inside?"

"Yes! There is. Is there a drugstore or some place in town that can develop it? Hopefully it's not so old that it's ruined."

"I know a place in town, the old apothecary. They still do it, though I'm not sure for how much longer," replied John.

"Here." Keith held the old Kodak out to him. "Go ahead. I'm going to check on a few more things. When you get back, we can finish up with Mom's paperwork."

John took the camera. "OK, sounds good. Be careful though, I'm not sure how safe it is. The barn has been in disrepair for quite some time."

"Sure thing, thanks bro."

After finding his Mom's camera, Keith felt the urge to make sure he hadn't missed anything. To check out those three planks. He grabbed his flashlight from the kitchen table and a small crowbar from Mom's toolbox at the top of the basement stairs. A blue-handled claw hammer lay next to it. He grabbed that too and returned to the barn. One by one he removed the heavy boards, revealing a musty, shallow crawlspace underneath. From his knees, he shined the flashlight inside. Cobwebs, dirt, and odd-shaped ends and pieces of wood left there from the original construction. Nothing unusual.

Sighing but satisfied he'd investigated everything thoroughly, he got up to leave. He was excited to see what was on that film. *I'm sure that's what she meant about the barn—the camera.* He would replace the planks later. On his way back to the house though, he stopped short. He did *not* look thoroughly, not under the floor. *One last time.* He walked back quickly, got down on his hands and knees, then leaned down. With his head fully inside the opening, he looked carefully, shining the beam all around this time. Off to the left, as if tossed there from the opening, he saw something. Oblong, dust-covered and wrapped in something—burlap. Straining to reach, he was able to pinch a corner of the coarse fabric between two fingers and drag it over, then he pulled it up. He unwrapped it slowly, suspecting what it was before he even saw it. A machete, the blade rusted from the middle to the tip. Blackish stains on the handle.

Keith looked up one last time through the opening above and into the steeple, so high up, then again at the machete, his hands trembling.

TWELVE

"It is going to be a few hours before they can develop that film," said John. He'd just returned from the apothecary.

"I'm surprised they'll have it done today, actually." Keith went to the kitchen table and picked up the machete, holding it out with two hands for John to see. "I found this under the floor in the barn."

John cocked his head to one side and took it from Keith, turning it over, inspecting it closely. "You found this *where?*"

"Hidden in the barn, under the floorboards. Right in the middle."

They sat down, and John set the machete back on the table between them. "You know, when you first started digging into all of this, I was pissed. Really pissed. But I held my tongue because you're my brother. And I guess there was some small part of me deep down inside that thought there might actually be something there. But I've come to think that there isn't. Even this..." he pointed at the machete, "...doesn't mean anything. And your timing has been bad, Keith. The worst. You haven't exactly earned the right around here to be dredging up old family matters anyway."

Keith dipped his head in acknowledgement. It was true.

"We'll see what's on the film. But none of it, even with this," again he pointed to the machete, "indicates that Gramp's death was anything other than an accident. I know that's where you've been going with this all along. We'll see what's on the photos. If there's nothing there, promise me you'll drop it, OK?"

"Agreed," Keith replied.

John nodded back. "Good."

"But...before I do, I'd like to have another chat with Tom. I don't feel like we explored everything as thoroughly as we could have the first time, and we've got some time to kill before we pick up the pictures. Can you at least give me that?"

"Holy cow, Keith, you're impossible!" he exclaimed. "Fine, but after that, we are done with it. OK? I'm getting tired of all this."

"OK. Thanks brother."

THIRTEEN

"Did you know my Mom was into photography?" John asked Tom.

They were back in Jane's living room. Keith was munching on a homemade blueberry scone from the pile in the middle of the coffee table.

"Honestly, I don't recall." said Tom. "I know she was always up to something. She loved horses, I know. April was always riding around on that overgrown stallion of hers. She'd ride it downtown to buy groceries, even."

"I remember!" said Jane, holding up her hand enthusiastically. "I remember her on that horse, and I remember her taking pictures of everything. She was so sad when she lost her camera."

"What do you mean, she 'lost' her camera?" Keith asked.

"I just remember one day after church, everyone was having donuts and coffee at the rectory and I overheard her say that her camera was gone. She thought someone took it. She seemed heartbroken. I tried to console her. It happened right around the time your grandfather died. I'm pretty sure Lydia ended up buying her a new one."

Jane was excited, leaning forward in her chair. It was clear she sensed John and Keith were digging into something and was sure she'd just given them critical information. She watched them expectantly, waiting for some form of validation, but they didn't oblige.

They stayed for thirty minutes more, and the conversation eventually turned to old town stories and the latest gossip. Keith announced they had to be leaving and thanked Jane and Tom for their hospitality once again. It was time to find out what was on that film.

After dropping John off, he went to the apothecary to pick up the developed pictures. As he was paying, the clerk, who looked well into his eighties, smiled at him. He was wearing a blue apron with a white nametag that read 'HELLO, My Name is Earl.'

"You know, that was some pretty old film. I'm surprised the photos came out so well," he said.

Keith glanced up and smiled as he handed the man his credit card. "Yeah, my mom took them, when she was a child. Kind of excited to see them."

"If you don't mind me asking," the man continued, "are those from the old Conway ranch?"

"Yes…why, did you recognize anything? Or anyone?" Keith was interested in seeing what the elderly gentleman had to say.

"Well, the house of course. Most people knew about the Conway Farm back then. There's a couple pictures of Jim in there."

"You knew my grandfather?"

The man chuckled. "Well, we weren't buddies, but I knew who he was. I was just a kid back then." He extended a thick envelope across the counter.

Keith opened it immediately and began thumbing through. There were eleven black and white photos, with surprisingly clear resolution given the age of the film. There was a photo of a young girl that looked suspiciously like a very young Jane Cranmore, playing in the yard. A few of Gram and Gramp. In one of those, Gramp was trying to spray Gram with a water hose—most likely posed but a great photo, nonetheless. Another of an obviously pregnant brown and white guernsey cow out in the field, and one of their Mom's stallion, Flapjack. One photo showed a man standing on the front stairs to their house, looking back and smiling.

Keith put his index finger on the photo. "Do you recognize this guy?"

He took a pair of spectacles from his apron pocket, out them on and leaned forward, almost straining. "He might have been one of their tenants. Or a handyman." He picked it up and held it closer, studying it. "You know what, I know who this is. That's Greg Donovan. Yes, he was a tenant. A real piece of work, that one." He placed the photo back on the counter.

"What do you mean?" asked John.

"Well, the story goes that this guy Donovan was the town drunk, always getting into trouble. He was homeless for a while, and nobody liked him. Even the kids made fun of him. Jim, your grandfather, he felt bad for the guy. I guess they used to run together when they were kids. But anyways, Jim renovated the house with those apartments of his, and he offered one of the rooms to Donovan as long as he promised to clean himself up and get a job. He let him cover his rent for the first few months doing odd jobs and such around the farm. But he never did clean up, and after a while Jim had to throw him out. It was big news back then, in such a small town. Jim threw all his stuff out in the street. Later on, someone threw a brick through Jim's front window. The sheriff suspected it was Donovan, but no one could prove anything. He hung around for a while, back in the streets. Then he disappeared, not sure where he went after that."

Keith paused in thought. "Sir, about when did Donovan disappear? Was it around the time of my grandfather's death? Do you recall what happened to my grandfather?"

The man took off his spectacles, folded them and put them back in his apron. "I remember what happened. A terrible accident; everyone was sad to see your grandfather go. He was a good man. And yes, I suppose it was right around that time."

THE BARN

FOURTEEN

Keith spread the photos out on the kitchen table as he explained to John everything the apothecary owner told him.

There were a few pictures from the neighborhood and around town. An unsuspecting man on the sidewalk pushing a baby carriage. A picture of a woman on the street. A black Model-T driving by.

The last was a closeup of Gramp sitting in lawn chair, just in front of the barn. Not one of Mom's best shots—Gramp was blurry. The focus was on the barn instead.

"Where is that picture that Tom gave us?" asked Keith.

"It's on the counter, hold on," said John.

He walked over and took it from atop a small pile of unopened mail near the bread box, the old photo of the kids down at the river.

He handed it to Keith, who placed it beside the photo of Donovan from April's camera. He was much younger at the time, but it was unmistakably the same person.

"Tom said this kid's name was Greg something...It definitely looks like the same guy, Greg Donovan," Keith said.

John nodded. "Yeah, it does. I guess Gramp knew Donovan for years."

Keith was nodding as well. "Listen, I don't believe his death was an accident, John. I think he was murdered. I figure whoever did it killed him with the machete in the barn, dragged him over, and impaled him on the sickle bar mower. To make it look like he fell down the stairs and landed on it. Then they hid the machete under the floor."

John regarded him carefully. "Slow down, brother. I agree that a hidden machete is a strange thing, but it's not enough. It probably wasn't even hidden. It could have just been dropped and left there by accident, by whoever built the barn."

Keith sighed. "Yes, I understand. But there was something up with those floorboards—there were three that seemed a different color than the rest. It was really hard to tell but once I blew off all the dust, I noticed. It's what led me to pull them up in the first place. I don't think it was left there by accident. This Greg Donovan, his tenant...heck, Gramp threw him out on the street. The brick through the window! He had motive, John. We need to find out more about him."

"You said that after we look at these, as long as there's no real evidence on the film, then you would let it go," John replied. "Are you saying that you won't?"

"No, I won't. Not yet, anyway. I think there IS evidence here, that's my point."

John looked at him angrily, got up from his chair abruptly and left the room.

The photos from the neighborhood stuck out. The three of the strange woman were sequential. Keith walked to the front door, opened it, and looked outside, holding one of the photos out in front.

Mom took this photo from the porch, Keith realized. He returned and placed the photo back with the other two. *There she is walking on the other side of the road. In the next one she is turning to cross the street, and in this one,*

Keith put his forefinger on the photo, *it looks like she is headed toward the house.*

He looked closer. The way she wore her hair, draped over one side of her face—as if she was trying to hide something. He looked at all three again. In one photo, the wind was blowing her hair back a bit, revealing a scar underneath. He yelled to his brother in the living room. "John, I think this is the girl from Tom's photo. Margot?"

After a moment, John poked his head through the doorway. "Conjecture, conspiracy, coincidence," he replied irritatingly. "Who cares who she is. In and of itself, it means nothing. Think about it! An unreliable tenant. A woman on the street. There is no way to connect any of these dots. It's all random and unconnected Keith! I can't explain the machete, but to me, the rest of it is bullshit. I never thought I'd say something like this about *you*, but you're getting way too emotional about all of it. Time to let it go, brother. We have more important things to attend to right now."

"OK, maybe you're right. But why not bring the matter to the police, see if it's something they want to look into? We don't even need to be part of it. Give them the machete, see if they could test it for DNA. They might find hair samples from an old brush of his, or something…"

"Keith, listen. This sleepy, small-town precinct wouldn't be interested. Not without a lot more and much better evidence, at least. And even if we found some hair samples, how would they know for sure they were Gramp's? Just let it go, brother."

"John, don't you want to know the truth? Or at the least, to eliminate the possibility he was murdered?"

"No," John replied strongly, leaving the doorway.

Two days passed. Keith asked around in town about the picture of the woman in front of their house, and the one in Tom's photo. After striking out several times, an elderly lady with a pipe in front of *Ye Olde Smoke Shoppe* confirmed the two girls were one in the same, though her name wasn't Margot or Melanie. It was Melissa. Melissa Johnson, Sheriff Johnson's daughter. Old Clyde and his wife both passed away some 30 years ago, she told him.

It should have been a revelation of sorts—this woman being the daughter of the Sheriff. But even after everything he'd uncovered, John was still right. It had been too easy for Keith to think all these things were somehow related. And maybe there were some connections, but there was still no real proof of anything. If there had been, Keith knew John would be with him on it. Experiencing a sudden sense of failure, Keith decided to give up and put it all behind him.

The brothers focused on funeral preparations and finishing up the estate issues. Keith picked out a few things to take home to Texas, boxing up others to ship back. Gramp's old gramophone, antique cookware from Ireland passed down through the family. A few other personal items with sentimental value. John kept mom's camera—Keith let him have it, though he secretly wanted it as well.

Breakfast, coffee. Walks downtown. Talks with the family lawyer. John met with a potential tenant for one of the apartments—that seemed promising. Through it all, Keith remained upset he'd been unable to reconcile it all, continually pushing it to the back of his mind. But it kept creeping back.

They got around to splitting up the family photos. John told Keith to go ahead and take what he wanted. There were several albums and three boxes, in addition to the one they'd already gone through.

Keith took the ones he wanted, being careful to leave some of the good ones for his brother. After a while, John came back in the room.

"Hey, I just got a call from the apothecary. Old Earl said there was one last picture from mom's camera that was left in the machine by accident. Says we can come pick it up."

Keith had just spent two hours going through family photos. He didn't feel much like going into town for one more but decided to anyway.

"I'll go pick it up then," he said.

"OK," replied John.

When he got there, Earl handed him a small envelope and smiled warmly. "I heard about you mom. My condolences."

"Thanks Earl, I appreciate it."

Back in the car, he started the engine and opened the envelope. Inside was another photo of Gramp, sitting in a lawn chair in front of the barn. It looked like a duplicate, or a shot taken right after or before the other one from the batch. And just like the other photo, Gramp was out of focus, and the barn was sharp. But there was something else, and it was unnerving. A good distance behind and to the left of his grandfather, a ghostly face peered around the far corner of the barn. A woman's face, partly in shadow and almost unnoticeable, but recognizable due to the dark diagonal scar across her left cheek and temple.

"Holy shit, Melissa Johnson?" Keith thought out loud.

Staring straight into the camera. Straight at Mom. Creepy as hell. She must have noticed Mom approaching and hidden, not realizing she'd be captured in the photo. Or maybe she was spying on Gramp. Mom saw she was there when she took the photo, that's why she took it.

Did Gramp have an affair? Why would he? Melissa Johnson was unsightly, with that scar. *Why would he do such a thing? He wouldn't.* Keith drove home quickly, gripping the steering wheel tightly. He went straight to the spare bedroom closet and pulled the box out, reaching beneath the photos for Gramp's yearbook. Opening it, he found the page with Gramp's photo and carefully picked at the smiley face sticker next to the *'I love you'* message. With his fingernail he caught the edge and slowly began to remove it. The old sticker had become brittle, flaking off in small pieces. The glue remained on the page, leaving a round, dark yellow circle in its place. But it was not so dark that he couldn't read the name penned underneath. *Melissa.*

At first, he wanted to show the photo to John. This could be part of the puzzle. But he realized it would only complicate things further between them. He kept thinking—Gramp was out of focus in the photos because Mom was focusing on Melissa, who was hiding near the corner of the barn. She was probably scared that Melissa saw her take the photo and might confront her about it, try to take the film. It's why she hid the camera. It was something she could use later, leverage. His Mom was just a child at the time, and suspicions of her father cavorting with a woman on the side likely scared her. She probably didn't know what else to do. It's why she claimed her camera was stolen, why she kept it a secret all those years. *Maybe.*

But Keith wouldn't tell John. His brother had already put it all behind him, and Keith had promised to let it go. It was selfish of him to keep trying to involve him. Everything he'd uncovered to-date indicated there'd been foul play, and all signs pointed to his former tenant. He was sure of it. So, he said it to himself instead, in his mind, where it wouldn't hurt anyone. *It's possible that Gramp was unfaithful to Gram. And I think Donovan did it. I think he murdered our grandfather…*

FIFTEEN

A large crowd joined them at the funeral. John delivered her eulogy. It was emotional; he had always been good with words, and there were so many beautiful things to say about their Mom. She'd led a difficult, but in many other ways, a wonderful life. Many from around town came to pay their respects. John seemed to know most of them. Keith did not.

Afterwards, a smaller group joined them at the house. Everyone brought a dish. Jane and Tom were there.

"Thanks for coming, and for having us over this past week. It was nice to reminisce," said John.

"Of course. And I'm so sorry for your loss, both of you poor, poor boys," lamented Jane.

Keith couldn't get past Jane's exaggerated nature—her entire personality was overdone, overcooked. Everything she did and said seemed fake. It was *possible* she really meant all of it, that she wasn't fake at all. Maybe that's just how she was wired. It was unfortunate, either way.

"Tom, I have a question," asked Keith. "About the girl from the photo you gave us, the one that Gram hurt. I found out her name was Melissa, not Margot. Melissa Johnson. Whatever became of her? Is she still alive?"

Tom looked bewildered, then looked around the living room, as if to get his bearings. "Johnson? Huh… My memory just isn't what it used to be. But now I remember—old Sherriff Johnson did have a daughter. Yes, that was her. I just never put two and two together… The Johnsons had the property next to your grandparents, right next to this place on the south side." He pointed left. "They both passed a long time ago. I figured someone else just bought the place. Not sure who. I think we'd've known if his daughter was still living there."

John shook his head. "I don't think she is. I've only ever seen a young woman coming and going from there. I don't know her, never talked to her." He and Keith exchanged glances. "If Melissa Johnson is still alive and does in fact live there, she's a total recluse."

Keith felt suddenly uneasy. Could she be the small, shadowy figure he'd seen in the window from the steeple? After all this time, could she still be haunting his family?

SIXTEEN

The last of the visitors came and went. Many kind words, some tears. John and Keith thanked the minister, who drove off as they began cleaning up.

"I'm going to go for a walk before bed," Keith said.

John was just putting away the last of the dishes. "OK, sure. I'll leave the door unlocked."

"Thanks."

He'd resigned himself to dropping his inquisition. His mom's funeral had brought a certain level of closure to it all, and he'd gained some level of serenity. But before he returned to Texas, he wanted to check on this one last thing.

Keith walked the quarter mile to the neighboring house. On the way, he wondered what he would say to her, if she was there. *She won't be there. She's probably dead.* She would be so old now. *But that doesn't matter.* He walked up the front porch steps and knocked.

He waited, then knocked again. Louder this time. Movement in the side window, a curtain being held aside. It was too dark to see who it was. Then, the sound of a deadbolt being retracted and a cackling voice: "Come in, it's open."

She wore a simple black dress, in a wheelchair. A lattice veil shadowed her face. Behind her, a young woman in the kitchen holding a hand towel watched, appearing concerned. The woman John had seen.

"You'll have to forgive me. It takes a while to get around these days. You're John Conway's brother, yes?"

"Yes, I'm Keith," he replied. "And you are Ms. Johnson, yes?" He felt immediately awkward. The old, broken woman in front of him couldn't possibly have had an affair with his Gramp, could she? He shouldn't even bring it up. "I...wanted to ask you some questions, if that's OK. About my grandfather. About one of his old tenants. I know it's late, but..."

She grabbed the wheels and backed up, giving him room to walk inside. "Yes, my name is Melissa Johnson." She looked back at the young woman. "Alice, you can go home now. Everything is fine."

The young woman folded the hand towel and placed it on the counter. "OK Ms. Johnson. Call me if you need anything." She gave Keith a long look, sizing him up, then left. He closed the door behind her.

He followed Melissa into the den, where she wheeled her chair around to face him, surprisingly spry. He remained standing.

"I am sorry for your loss, Keith. Please pass my regards on to John. I would have been there, but..." She tapped her wheelchair armrest.

"Thank you, I will," he replied hesitatingly.

"So, what can I do for you, Keith?"

He shifted on his feet, still feeling uncomfortable. "My grandfather...I know you knew him back in the day. I know there was an altercation between you and my grandmother..."

"She gave me this," said Melissa, pulling back her veil. She raised her voice as she said it. Among the numerous lines and wrinkles on her face, the scar looked less pronounced than in the photos. "It ruined my life."

She settled back into her wheelchair, dropping the veil.

"I'm sorry."

"But that's not why you're here. Go ahead, ask me your questions."

Keith sat in a threadbare armchair across from her. "That was you in the window the other day. When I was in the steeple."

She cocked her head. "You mean you were up there, in your mom's barn? You saw me? What a strange question… Not even a question, actually. That's my bedroom window. I look out of it occasionally. You know, as people do…" She pointed over her shoulder at the staircase. "I may be in a wheelchair, but I can still manage the stairs twice a day. It takes forever. You know, I would see your mother in the steeple from time to time, when she was young. Always taking pictures. But what does this have to do with James?"

Hearing her use his grandfather's first name seemed wrong. Too personal. It made him angry. Melissa shrunk back in her wheelchair, holding up both hands defensively. She was afraid. He realized he'd made fists with both hands and could feel the heat as blood rushed from his chest, up his neck. His heart was pounding. He quickly unclenched his fists.

"I'm sorry, please don't take it the wrong way. I'm not feeling well, you know, the funeral." Awkward again; it was all he could think to say.

Melissa relaxed. "OK, well it's getting late. Is there anything else?"

Keith forced a smile. "Tom Cranmore gave me an old photo the other day—my grandfather is in it, so is my grandmother. And you. And…there's another boy in the photo, his name was Greg Donovan. Do you remember him?"

"Old Greg? Who doesn't remember Greg. He was a bastard, that one."

"So I've heard. But what I want to know is…do you think he ever had reason to hurt my grandfather? I mean, do you know where he went about the time my grandfather died?"

She regarded him carefully. "Why do you want to know?"

"Because I don't think my grandfather's death was an accident. I think someone killed him, and then covered it up."

Melissa continued to look straight at him, gauging him. A palpable silence filled the room. Finally, she responded.

"Greg Donovan might have been a bastard, but he didn't kill your grandfather. He couldn't have. My father arrested him weeks earlier for robbing Rob McCutcheon's general store. He didn't get out until at least a month after your grandfather's accident. Then he left town for good, went to the big house. He died in there." Then, with finality, she added, "and your grandfather's death was an accident. Everyone knows that."

As he listened, Keith felt a curious relief overcome him. Relief that his suspicions were unfounded, that it was all just coincidence.

"Thank you, Ms. Johnson," he said respectfully. "That's very helpful.

She smiled curtly, placing her hands on the chair wheels. "My pleasure, Keith. Now, if that's all, I need to get ready for bed. Again, I'm sorry for your loss."

He got up to go. "Have a good evening."

But he couldn't leave yet. She'd been more than willing to talk…He could ask one more question. Get closure on one simple thing.

He turned back to face her. "Did you have an affair with him? With my grandfather?"

She stiffened again, saying nothing at first. Another long, loud silence. Then she began to speak, in a dry whisper. "I loved him. I loved him, Keith. But I couldn't have him. There was a chance at one time, I know, but my life was ruined at such an early age. Never able to love anyone again because of my scarred face. Never to be loved. I was selfish…"

He interrupted her. "What are you saying? Did you, or not? I just want to know. I'm not going to tell anyone else. I just want to know. For me." He said it firmly.

She continued, head off to one side now, as if in reverie. "I sent him a note one day, for him to meet me in his barn. I snuck in and he was already there. I told him I loved him, that Lydia didn't deserve him. That I would take care of him like no one could. But he was so upset with me, told me to leave him alone. Leave his family alone. He threatened to call my father if I didn't leave." She took a deep breath, then went on. "But I wouldn't listen, I couldn't. I ran up the stairs. I threatened to jump out the window. He laughed at me then, which made me cry. I remember, he said *'all you'll do is break your leg, and then I'll have to take you to the hospital. Come down and go home,'* he said…"

Keith was confused, nervous, not knowing what to think. He urged her to continue.

"That's when I noticed the machete, on the workbench. I wasn't thinking, I was so overcome. I held the blade to my throat and told him I'd rather die than be without him. He came up the stairs slowly, I remember this part as if it were yesterday. He held out his hand and said, *'Melissa, we can talk about it, see what's possible. Maybe we can work something out. Just give me the knife.'*"

Keith's eyes were wide, his hands in fists again, but she didn't notice this time. She paused again and began to sob.

"So, I held it out to him. I didn't truly want to kill myself; I was just trying to get him to say what I wanted to hear. As he approached me, I asked him to promise me we'd be together. Somehow. But he wouldn't say it. I put the blade to my neck again and kept backing up, until I was at the edge of that big hole in the floor up there. He kept coming, I could tell he was going to try to take the machete from me. I was leaning up against the railing, and it started to give—I was about to fall and then thought, good. And at that moment, I really did want to die. I leaned backwards even more, breaking the railing. He reached me at that moment, grabbing my arm and pulling me towards him, back from the edge. He saved me. That's when I realized, at some point I'd taken the blade away from my throat. And then there he was, my poor James, standing at the broken railing with the machete stuck in his chest. It went in *so far*, My God, I don't know how… He had a confused look on his face. He went down on his knees, then toppled over the side and landed on the floor below."

Melissa was crying. Years of pain breaking through. Keith was in complete shock and pale as a ghost and. Tears began to roll down his face uncontrollably.

"I cannot change the past," she continued, in between the sobs. "I've had to live with this my whole life. I regret what I did. If I'd just accepted my plight, my place in life, none of this would have come to pass. I was a young fool filled with love and rage. I shouldn't have covered it all up—I should have told the truth. It was an accident, but it wouldn't have happened at all if I'd left well enough alone."

She stopped to catch her breath. "I fixed the railing and moved him over to the sickle bar. He was so heavy. I tried to clean up the blood, but it had soaked into the floor. There was a pry bar and claw hammer upstairs. I used those to remove the floorboards, and then I hid the machete underneath. I pulled the nails out of the planks, flipped them over, and nailed them back. It felt like I was in there all morning. When I was finishing, I heard Lydia calling his name. I just made it out of the barn before she went in. I heard her screams as I ran through the woods."

She was speaking faster now, eager to get it all out. To finally tell the truth.

"I never expected my lie to last this long. I always thought that my father knew I did it, but he never said anything to me. He never asked me about it. I think that's why my parents sent me away to live with my aunt for all those years. But I never spoke of it to anyone. Until this moment. Now I am an *old* fool, filled with regret, waiting for death."

She looked up at him and pulled the veil back again, over the top of her head. Tears streaked her wrinkled, scarred face. "I am so, so very sorry, Keith. I know that doesn't mean much to you right now. These terrible things cannot be undone. But I am truly sorry."

He was incredulous. He never thought she might be his grandfather's killer. Did Mom know Melissa did it? If so, why hadn't she told anyone? When she said, *'It's in the barn,'* was she talking about her camera, or the machete? Or both? All the signs had pointed to Donovan. Maybe she only suspected...or maybe it meant nothing—she was delusional, and it was just a weird coincidence. *I'll never really know.* What was he to do? Call the police? There should be closure. For John...for the town. For *him*. He wanted so badly to be angry, to feel the rage he knew he should be experiencing at this moment. *Of course* the investigation found Gramp's death to be an accident—the investigator was none other than the killer's father! Old Clyde knew she did it, and he took part in the cover up. But the rage didn't come. Instead, he was experiencing an overwhelming sadness. For his grandfather, for John and his mother. Sad for himself. And strangely, sad for Melissa, even.

"Thank you for telling me, Ms. Johnson." It was all he could come up with in the moment. There wasn't much he could say or do to her that karma hadn't already brought to bear. So he turned away, wiping his face dry with his shirtsleeve. He walked out of the room, through the front door, and back towards the house.

SEVENTEEN

John was still up when he got back, watching television and sipping from a tumbler of scotch. He looked over as Keith came in. "Hey there."

"Hey."

"I forgot to ask, what was on that last photo?"

Keith took his phone from his pocket and looked thoughtfully at the cracked screen, then walked over and set it on the coffee table. He sat next to his brother on the couch. "It was nothing, really. Just another picture of the barn. It was out of focus. I tossed it."

"Huh," John replied, turning his attention back to the television. "How was your walk?"

Keith sighed and stared blankly at the TV. The adrenaline from his confrontation with Melissa was now gone, leaving him drained. It would be all too easy to tell John. There was a part of him that was screaming it was the right thing to do. *He deserves to know.* Another part was whispering in his ear, calmly, that he should let it go. Sometimes, the easy thing comes cloaked in the guise of what is right. Maybe karma was enough.

"It was fine, brother. Everything is fine."

AUTHORS' NOTE

Although the characters and events that unfold in this mystery novella are fictitious, several aspects of the story are based upon real places, including the barn itself.

ABOUT THE AUTHORS

DOUG CAMPBELL and JOHN CASEY grew up together in southern New Hampshire. The two took divergent career paths, but remain close friends. Campbell is an entrepreneur, an executive financial consultant to the life sciences industry, and owns and operates real estate properties. He is a former naval officer and enjoys playing the guitar and a good murder mystery. Casey is a novelist and Pushcart Prize-nominated poet. He is the author of *The Devolution Trilogy*, *Raw Thoughts: A Mindful Fusion of Poetic and Photographic Art,* and *Meridian: A Raw Thoughts Book*. A Veteran combat and test pilot, Casey also served as a diplomat and international affairs strategist at U.S. embassies in Germany and Ethiopia, the Pentagon, and elsewhere. He is passionate about fitness, nature, and the human spirit. For more information on John Casey and his writing, visit https://johnjcasey.com.

Printed in Dunstable, United Kingdom